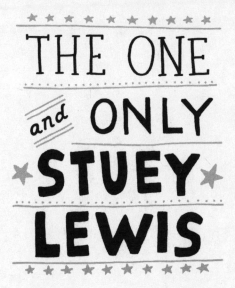

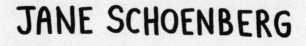

JANE SCHOENBERG

STORIES from the **SECOND** GRADE

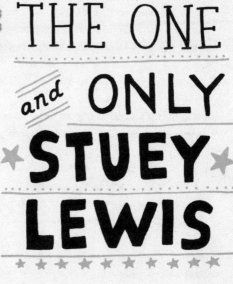

THE ONE
and ONLY
STUEY
LEWIS

pictures by

CAMBRIA EVANS

SQUARE FISH

Farrar Straus Giroux
New York

SQUARE
FISH

An Imprint of Macmillan

Library of Congress Cataloging-in-Publication Data

Schoenberg, Jane, 1952–

The one and only Stuey Lewis / Jane Schoenberg ; pictures by

Cambria Evans.

p.   cm.

Summary: Stuey Lewis makes his way through second grade facing
reading problems, pulling off a great Halloween caper, joining a soccer
team, and more with the help of family, friends, and a special teacher.

ISBN 978-1-250-02216-5

[1. Schools—Fiction.   2. Teachers—Fiction.   3. Family life—
Fiction.]   I. Evans, Cambria, ill.   II. Title.

PZ7.S3652One 2011   [E]—dc22   2010022312

Originally published in the United States by Farrar Straus Giroux

First Square Fish Edition: September 2012

Square Fish logo designed by Filomena Tuosto

mackids.com

2   4   6   8   10   9   7   5   3   1

AR: 2.9 / LEXILE: 410L

For Steven, my one and only
—J.S.

For Soren, Elsa, Barek, and William
—C.E.

Contents

I wake up and decide to have a stomachache that's so bad I have to stay in bed.

"Hey, Stu-pid!" yells my big brother, Anthony, who's four years older than me. "Move it or you'll miss the bus!"

I never let it slide when Anthony calls me stupid. The very least I do is tell Mom. But this time, I don't say a word. I don't move. I don't get dressed. I don't go downstairs.

It's Wednesday, French toast day. The middle-of-the-school-week day, when Mom makes a special breakfast.

Mom walks into my room. "What's going on, Stuey?" she asks.

"Stomachache," I say in my whiniest voice. "I'm too sick to go to school."

She puts her hand on my forehead. She gives me the real once-over. "You don't have a fever. You look fine. Get dressed and come downstairs. Your French toast is getting cold."

I eat three pieces of French toast. I know it doesn't look good for someone with a stomachache. But I can't help it, Mom makes the best French toast. Maybe she won't notice.

"I guess your stomach must be feeling better," says Mom.

Oh well. Maybe if I eat another piece, I'll *really* get sick.

"Come on, Stu," says Anthony. "We have to get going. We don't want to miss the bus."

But of course I want to miss the bus.

I'll do anything to miss it. I'll clean my room. I'll clean Anthony's room. I'll even clean the whole house. Bingo! That's it! Mom's always wanted a housecleaner.

"Hey, Mom! How about if I stay home today? I'll clean the whole house for you."

She rolls her eyes.

"First it was a stomachache, and now you want to clean the house?" She feels my forehead again. "Maybe you're sick after all."

I try to look as green as possible.

"Okay, Stuey, what's going on?" she asks.

"I'm sick of school," I tell her.

Anthony snorts. "Hey, Stupi—" He catches himself just in time. "How can you be sick of school? It's only our third day."

I decide not to tell the truth. How can I tell them my awful secret? How can I tell them, I've been in second grade for two whole days and I'm still wicked slow at reading. Everyone said the lightbulb would go on by now. It's bad enough it didn't happen last year or over the summer. But if the kids figure out I'm still no good at it, or even worse the teacher does, I'm toast.

"Last call for the bus, Bro," says Anthony. And he pulls me out the door.

I walk into my classroom. It's actually full of very cool stuff. A person could have a lot of fun in here. If that person already knew how to read.

My teacher, Ms. Curtis, is writing the morning message. She wants us to call her Ginger. Mom thinks that's very modern. I think it's dumb. We're the first class she's ever taught. She says we have a lot to learn from each other. And she wants us all to be good friends. If she was my good friend, I could tell her my secret. But she's not.

"Hey, Stuey," says Will. "Dad's taking me fishing on Saturday. Want to come?"

"Thanks," I say. "I'll ask Mom and tell you tomorrow."

Me and Will Fishman have been best friends forever. He shares his dad with me 'cause mine moved away. Today, Will is the only good thing about second grade.

I always feel better when I share yucky stuff with him. So I decide to tell him my secret. On the count of three, get ready . . . One, two . . .

"And after fishing, we get to go to Paperback Heaven!" Will is all pumped up. "They're having a giant sale. If you buy one book, you get one free! Dad said I could get five books. So I can actually get ten. Maybe you can get ten, too."

My stomach does a little flip. There's no way I'm going to Paperback Heaven with Will. No way at all.

"I just remembered something, Will,"

I say. "Mom says I have to clean my room on Saturday."

"Well, can you ask her anyway?"

"Okay," I say.

I feel really guilty now. Not telling the truth is not getting easier. But what else can I do?

Will was reading way back in pre-

school. He was reading when he was born. He's like a reading monster. He eats books up. Humongous fat ones, even. He's been real patient, too. He's been waiting years for me to catch up and read as fast as he does. I just can't let him know it still hasn't happened yet.

"Good morning, everyone. Please join me on the meeting rug." Ms. Curtis is waiting in her rocking chair, by the easel with the morning message.

"Just follow my pointer and we'll all read today's message together," she says.

I look around. If everyone is looking at her pointer, I'm safe. 'Cause then no one will be looking at my lips, which definitely won't be moving.

Hello, Second Graders,
This morning we have D.E.A.R.
That stands for Drop Everything
And Read.

Our D.E.A.R. buddies will be
Mr. Stone's sixth graders.
Later we will have gym. Let's talk
about how D.E.A.R. works.

Ginger

"Nice reading, friends," says Ms. Curtis. "Does anyone have any questions about D.E.A.R.?"

"I know all about deer," says Sam. "I'm a deer expert, Ginger. My grandpa lives in the country. He's got tons of deer that live near him."

"Duh," says Lilly Stanley. "Ginger doesn't mean that kind of deer, Sam. She was talking about the D.E.A.R. program. Right, Ginger?"

That Lilly is a big know-it-all. Only she doesn't *know* how annoying *she* is. I almost tell her, too, 'cause Sam looks really embarrassed. But I'm trying very hard not to be noticed. And that's not always so easy for me.

"We'd love to have you tell us about deer, Sam. Perhaps at our next sharing time?" Ms. Curtis smiles at him.

Then she gives Lilly one of those teacher looks. Not the happy kind, either.

"Friends, listen up, here's the number one rule in this classroom. Put-downs are not allowed. It is never okay to

embarrass anyone. Understand? We all need to feel comfortable here."

Everybody nods. But I'm not taking any chances. I'm keeping my secret all to myself.

Hello, Second Graders,
This morning we have
D.E.A.R.
That stands for
Drop Everything And Read.
Our D.E.A.R. buddies will
be Mr. Stone's sixth graders.
Later we will have gym.
Let's talk about how
D.E.A.R. works.
Ginger

Ms. Curtis explains how D.E.A.R. works. Every second grader gets a sixth grader for a reading buddy. For fifteen minutes we share books with them. We have D.E.A.R. every Wednesday for the whole year. It's supposed to be fun.

Fun? For some kids, maybe. For Will, definitely. For me, *No way!*

Then she gives us the names of our buddies.

"Stuey Lewis's buddy is Steven Roy."

Will gives me the thumbs-up. But my stomach does an upside-down roller-coaster ride. I think I'm gonna lose Wednesday's special breakfast. For real, this time. No lie.

"Are you feeling all right, Stuey?" Ms. Curtis asks. "You look a little green."

"I feel a little green," I say.

A few kids laugh. But my stomach feels too shaky to care. Steven Roy is Anthony's best friend. They tell each other everything. No way is any secret safe with Steven Roy. No way is he *ever* gonna be my reading buddy.

Ms. Curtis shushes the other kids. "What did we just talk about, friends? Now pick out a book to share with your reading buddy."

Then she asks me to come over to her rocking chair. "Do you need to go to the nurse?" she whispers.

"Yes," I say. "I guess I'll just have to miss D.E.A.R. time today."

She gives me one of those teacher looks. The maybe-something-else-is-going-on kind.

"Is there anything you want to tell me, Stuey?" she asks.

"Well, I'd like you to change my reading buddy."

"How come, Stu?"

She seems to really care. It almost makes me want to call her Ginger. It almost makes me want to tell the truth. But not the whole truth. So I decide to tell a piece of it.

"I won't be comfortable with him."

"Are you sure?" she asks.

I nod my head yes.

"Do you want to tell me why?" she asks.

I shake my head no.

And do you know what? She doesn't ask any more questions. She just gets up and gets her list.

"I could switch your partner with Sam's. Would you be willing to give Natalie Archer a try?" she asks.

"I guess so," I say. "Can I go to the nurse now?"

She gives me another one of those looks. But she lets me go anyway. *Yes! I'm safe till next Wednesday!*

My stomach starts feeling better when I get to Mrs. Cotton's office.

"What's the problem, Stuey?" she asks.

"Too many pieces of French toast," I say. "But I'm gonna feel better in time for gym class."

She puts her hand on my forehead. Then she gives me a wink.

"I'm sure you are," she says. "Want to lie down for a bit?" Then she fluffs up a pillow for my tired head.

Keeping a secret is a lot of work. I close my eyes and have a little rest.

"Hi, are you Stuart?" A girl with dark hair and glasses is standing by my cot.

She's got a book in her hand. "I'm Natalie, your reading buddy."

Relax, I say to myself. She's only a dream. I pinch myself, but guess what? She isn't!

"Want to hear a story? It might make you feel better," she says.

"Do *I* have to read?" I ask.

"No," she says. "You just get to rest. This is one of my old favorites. It always makes me feel better. Maybe it will help you, too."

And then, Natalie Archer, my D.E.A.R. buddy, begins to read.

I close my eyes and feel my crowded thoughts slowing down. I've just bought another day. My secret's still safe.

I was right about Steven Roy having loose lips. He blabbed to Anthony at lunch about my trip to the nurse and Anthony blabbed to Mom. So now she's rethinking Wednesday's special breakfasts. And she's gonna monitor how much I eat. All because Steven Roy can't keep his mouth shut. I knew he couldn't be my reading buddy.

"You look like you're feeling great this morning, Stuey," says Ms. Curtis when I walk into my classroom the next day. "Want to help write the morning message?"

"I'd love to help, Ginger!" says Lilly. "I'm an excellent writer."

For once I'm happy to have that annoying girl in my class.

"Thank you, Lilly, but I asked Stuey," says Ms. Curtis.

"I'm happy to give my turn to Lilly,"

I say. I give them both my best smile. "I can do it another day."

"That's very friendly of you, Stuey," Ms. Curtis says.

I can't tell which kind of teacher look she's giving me, but she hands Lilly a blue marker.

"Hey, Stuey," says Will. "Did you ask your mom about Saturday?"

I take a deep breath. "I can go fishing. But I'm not sure she'll let me go to the bookstore," I tell him.

"I don't get it, Stu. What's going on?" he asks.

I take another deep breath. It's now or never. I'm gonna tell him.

But then Ms. Curtis calls, "Good morning, everyone, please come to meeting."

"Ms. Curtis is waiting, Will. We better get over there," I say.

"It's time to read the morning message," says Ms. Curtis. "Please follow my pointer."

Hello, Second Graders,
Happy Thursday!
Today's lunch is pizza.
We have library this morning.
Let's go over the rules.
Ginger

"I know all about the library rules," says Lilly.

"I'm sure you do, Lilly," says Ms. Curtis. "But the rules are a bit different for second graders. This year you get to take out four books."

"Cool!" yells Will. Then he turns a little red. Normally he's pretty quiet.

"You can pick any three books you

want," says Ms. Curtis. "Picture books or chapter books. Fiction books or non-fiction books. And your mom or dad can read them to you."

Yes! It's still okay for Mom to read to me! I look at my teacher. I give her my first real smile since school started.

"But you also have to pick a book that *you* can read. So here's the five-finger rule, for the fourth book. Open the book. Read the first sentence. If you get stuck on more than five words, put it back. That's a book for later. For now, try an easier book."

No! That is not okay. No way is any-body gonna see me taking out a baby

book. I roll my eyes at
Ms. Curtis.

"Don't worry." Ms. Curtis looks right at me. "I'll help each of you pick out the perfect book."

She's right. I don't need to worry. 'Cause I am *not* going to the library. Not now, not ever.

"Can everyone please line up at the door," says Ms. Curtis.

"Let's go, Stu." Will grabs my hand. He's hot to trot.

Only I don't move. My bottom is glued to the floor.

"Come on, Stuey." Will is losing his patience. "We only have twenty minutes in the library."

"You go ahead, Will," I say, and he lines up.

"Ginger." Lilly's voice gives me

an instant headache. "Stuey Lewis isn't lining up."

"Thanks, Lilly, I appreciate your concern," Ms. Curtis says. She walks over to me and leans down. "I'll be back in a minute, Stuey," she whispers. "Stay put, okay?"

I nod.

Then she walks to the front of the line, and everyone files out the door.

The room is very quiet. I think I am very alone. I think it's no fun to miss library. And I think I would like to go home. But mostly, I think the five-finger rule stinks.

I hear Ms. Curtis, but I hope that, if I keep my eyes closed, she'll go away.

"I'm your teacher, Stuey," she whispers. "But I'd like to be your friend, too."

I don't say a word. But she knows I'm listening 'cause I open my eyes.

"Friends trust each other. So I'm going to trust you with a big secret. Okay?"

"Okay," I say.

"I didn't learn how to read until second grade," Ms. Curtis says.

"No way," I say. "Not till then?"

"Worse, really," she says. "Not until the *end* of second grade. And not really well until the end of third."

"Wow," I say. "That must have been hard."

"Sometimes life *is* hard. But you have to try to make it work."

"I guess so," I say. "I have been trying."

"I know," she says. Then she puts her arm around me. "So, what's making life hard for you, Stu?" she asks.

And do you know what? I tell her.

"But, Stuey," she says. "You've only been in second grade for four days. I can't wave a magic reading wand to make it happen. I have to teach you. Not everyone in this class knows how to read well."

"But they all know how to read way better than me. Especially Will."

"Well, you're right about Will," she says. "He's one of the lucky ones. Every now and then someone gets it right away. But hardly anyone in this class reads as well as he does. Nearly all of us have to work at it." Then she gives me a little squeeze. "And for most kids it's fun."

I give her a kid's look. The kind that says, I don't believe you.

"Don't believe me, huh?" she asks.

She walks me over to the morning message. She starts pointing to words.

"Pizza," I say. "Hello. Second. Graders. Happy. Thursday."

She takes her pointer and waves it over my head.

"Stuey Lewis, Reading Wizard!" she says.

"But I remembered those words," I tell her. "That's not *real* reading."

Then she laughs. "Real reading *is* remembering words. And looking at pictures. And sounding out letters. Try this."

She grabs a little book from the book box.

I open it and take a deep breath.

"I see a robin in a tree.
I see a seagull in the sea.

I see a blue jay in the snow.
I look for birds and wave hello!"

We look at each other and smile.

"Hello, Reader," she says.

"Hello, Ginger," I answer.

We give each other a high five.

"Can this be my five-finger-rule book?" I ask.

"It's perfect," she says. "If you like, the two of us can choose the five-finger-rule book from here every week until you feel ready to pick one out at the library." She looks at the clock. "If you hurry, you still have time to go to the library and get your other books."

I give her the thumbs-up. Then I'm off to find Will, and the rest of my books.

After supper, I decide it's time to come clean with Will, so I give him a call.

"I can go to Paperback Heaven after we go fishing, but there's something I have to tell you. I don't think I'm ready for ten humongous fat books yet."

"That's okay, Stuey," says Will, "you will be soon enough."

And soon enough suddenly feels all right.

Okay, I admit it, if I had to choose between candy and my big brother, Anthony? I'd choose candy. Gummy bears, chocolate, licorice, you name it, I love it all. Except for that powdery stuff that turns the inside of your mouth blue. *Gross!*

For Anthony, it's soccer, for Will, it's books, and Mom's into flowers. But me? I'm all about candy. It's a no-brainer that October is my favorite month of the whole year, and I'm psyched that the final countdown to Halloween is almost over.

"Hey, Stu-pid!" Anthony yells. "Are

you in a trance? Breakfast is ready. Get moving!"

"Stupid, huh? Do *you* know what *today* is, Mr. Medulla Oblongata?" I say.

"Medulla what?"

I can always count on Will for supplying me with big words that mean sick stuff. Even if I can't read them, I still know them.

"Oblongata. It's the lower part of your brain. But since you don't have one—"

Anthony takes a step toward me.

"Mom!" I call.

"Stop teasing Stuey, Anthony!" she yells. "And hurry it up, boys!"

We slide up to the table and help ourselves to Mom's apple muffins.

"So, what *is* today, Stu?" Anthony asks.

"Friday, October twenty-ninth," I answer. "The day I reveal my Halloween Caper."

"Your Halloween what?"

"Caper, as in trick, prank, joke, gag. And I'll tell you a little secret," I whisper. "It's gonna be amazing."

"Oh, I'm sure it is." Anthony rolls his eyes. "Especially if it's anything like last year's."

You could hardly call last year's mess a caper. More like an innocent mistake. Our teacher sent home a note asking us to bring in special Halloween snacks. Only I couldn't read at all back then and didn't show it to my mom. So I brought in a baby garter snake. I even dressed him up with a ribbon, special-like, for Halloween.

He looked pretty cool, but some of the kids didn't think so. Who knew that they would start screaming and that the principal was scared of snakes, too?

"That's history," I tell him. "That will never happen again." 'Cause now I finally get that a silent *e* at the end of the word makes the vowel say its name. A snake will never be a snack again!

"This is gonna be way better than the lemonade stunt Will and me pulled off at the lake this summer, Anthony. And it even tops my Sweet Tooth Club idea that scored me the best desserts from the kids in my class last fall. You thought those were pretty cool, right?"

"Yeah," Anthony says, "I guess that dessert club thing was pretty impressive. So what is it already?"

"Will is sleeping over tonight," I say.

"He hears about it then, and if you're nice to me all day, maybe you can hear about it then, too."

"How do I know it'll be worth it? Why should I even care?"

"Because it's totally awesome and it won't work without you. That's how important your part is. Trust me, you'll love this one, and so will Steven, I promise."

"Boys, get your backpacks. The bus will be here soon." Mom hands us each a box. "Your Halloween muffins are all packed for school."

"Thanks, Mom. Did you put gummy snakes on top of mine?" I ask.

"Yes, Stuey. But I'm not sure it was such a good idea," she says.

Anthony groans.

I give them both a thumbs-up.

* * *

When I get to my classroom, there's a whole table full of sweets. I'm in Halloween heaven!

Will looks at my box. "I hope there's only food in there," he says.

"Don't worry. Are you set for tonight?"

"I can't wait to hear about the caper," he whispers.

"It's a beaut," I tell him.

"Friends, can you join me at morning meeting?" Ms. Curtis has freckles painted all over her face. Her red hair is in braids, and they're sticking straight out of her ears.

"Guess who I am?" she asks.

I have no clue.

"Pippi Longstocking!" shouts Lilly. "You look adorable, Ginger! But *I* think Pippi's braids should curl up, not out."

"Thank you for your comment, Lilly." Ms. Curtis has a lot of patience. "Let's read the morning message together."

Boo!
Happy almost Halloween!
We will read a ghost story
this morning.
We will have a party this afternoon.
What are you going to be for
Halloween?
Pippi

"I *was* going to be a princess. But now I think I'll be Pippi. Just like you!" says Lilly. "Only *my* braids will curl *up*," she adds.

I'd like to curl all of Lilly up. Then I'd like to throw her in the trash. But I can't say that out loud.

"I'm going to be a monster," says Sam.

"A dinosaur," says Nathan.

"A witch," says Rosa.

"An alien," says Omar.

"A ballerina," says Sashi.

"A wizard," says Will.

"And what about you, Stuey?" Ms. Curtis asks.

"It's a secret," I say.

"I bet I know," says Ms. Mouthy Lilly.

"I don't even know," Will says quickly. "So there's no way you could."

"Well, Stuey, your secret is safe for now," says Ms. Curtis. "Maybe you'll share it with us on Monday."

"Oh, I'll know before then, Ginger," says Lilly. "Because we live in the same neighborhood and I'll see him trick-or-treating on Sunday." She gives me her best smarty-pants look.

"Want to bet no one will know that I'm me?" I ask.

"Sure," she says. "What?"

"All of your Halloween candy," I say.

Everyone's dead silent. You can hear a pin drop, it's that quiet.

"Wow," says Will. "That must be *some* costume you've got."

I nod my head. Then I look at Lilly, straight in the eye. "Well?" I ask.

She doesn't say a word. Nada, zip, zilch, nothing.

"I don't know about the rest of you, but I'm ready for some shivers," says Ms. Curtis. "Let's have our ghost story in the library today. Everyone, please line up at the door."

For once Will doesn't rush to be first in line.

"You'll find out tonight," I whisper. "It's all part of the Great Halloween Caper."

"Were you really going to bet *all* of your candy?" he asks.

I nod my head. "I wouldn't have lost," I tell him.

"I believe you," he says. That's why Will is my best friend.

After library, Ms. Curtis chooses one of our treats for morning snack.

"Whose box is this?" she asks.

I raise my hand. A few of the kids

look worried as she opens the lid and laughs.

"Perfect!" she says. "Who wants a slimy snake snack?"

That Ms. Curtis is one cool teacher, even with red braids sticking out of her ears. She passes out Mom's apple muffins and gives me a big grin when she hands me one.

"You're really something, Stu," she says. "Thanks for bringing in this great treat."

"You're welcome," I say.

After school, Will comes home with me on the bus. Steven Roy comes home with Anthony. Mom calls this Best Friend Night. We do it once a month. Mom makes pizza, and Anthony and Steven make me and Will crazy. But not tonight. Tonight they are both in best-behavior mode. Guess I psyched Anthony up after all, and he and Steven can't wait to hear about the caper.

"There's one piece of pepperoni left," says Anthony. "Want it, Stu?"

I grab the pepperoni before he can change his mind.

"Are you feeling all right?" asks Mom. She puts her hand on his forehead.

"Anthony and I will help clean up," says Steven.

Mom's mouth drops open, and Will grins at me. He can't believe it, either. After dinner, Will and I get to pick what *we* want to watch on TV. There is no teasing, no fighting, no sign of trouble. I could get used to this.

"You boys have been awesome tonight," says Mom. "Want to stay up a little later? I'll make popcorn."

I fake a yawn. "I'm real tired, Mom."

"Me, too," says Will.

"Think we'll hit the sack," says Anthony.

"Early Frisbee game tomorrow," says Steven.

"Okay, boys," says Mom. "Spill it. What's going on?"

"Nothing," we all say at the same time. We try to look sweet and innocent. I don't think she believes us, but I can tell she really wants to.

"Okay, then," she says with a smile. "I'll see you all in the morning. Good night, boys."

I point to my watch. "Be here at exactly nine thirty," I whisper to Anthony and Steven when Will and I get to my room. Then I lock my bedroom door and drag the big box out from the back of my closet.

"What's in there?" Will asks.

"My Halloween costume," I say.

I start pulling things out. "Wigs, masks, hats, sheets. I have all kinds of cool stuff."

Will starts pawing through everything. "But, Stuey, there's stuff in here for more than one costume."

"Nine, to be exact," I say.

Will looks confused. "Nine? I don't get it."

"You will," I say, looking at my watch. "In about thirty seconds."

There's a quiet knock on my door, and I let Anthony and Steven in.

"Okay, hotshot, we're all ears," says Anthony, looking at the box of costumes. "What have you cooked up this time?"

"You know how Mom always takes Will and me trick-or-treating? Well, she said this year we can trick-or-treat with you guys and she won't come if we only go around the block. And don't cross any streets."

"No way," says Steven, "that's hardly any houses. Anthony, did you know about this?"

"Mom didn't say anything to me, honest," he says to Steven, and then he pulls me off my bed. "I've been nice to you all day for this? It's a stupid caper. Just like you."

"Hold on," I say. "You haven't heard the caper yet. I counted thirty houses around the block, if we go around once. But what if we go around three times?"

"Three times thirty is nincty," says Anthony. "But who's going to give us candy three times?"

"Everyone," I say. " 'Cause no one will know it's us again. We change costumes each time we go around, like chameleons. Pretty cool, huh?"

"Hey, Stu-pid, that's pretty smart," says Steven. "That's way more houses than Anthony and I could ever cover by ourselves." He's got a big grin on his face.

"Who are you calling stupid?" asks Anthony. Then he high-fives me and gives me a smile. The kind that says, little brothers can be okay. Maybe I wouldn't trade him for licorice after all. But I'm not so sure about chocolate.

"Wow," says Will. "You're incredible."

I take a bow. "I figure we'll be eating Halloween candy till Christmas, at least."

Then we get down to business. I take my three costumes from the box: knight, ghost, pirate.

"You guys start out in your own costumes," I explain. "Then you'll wear the two you choose from this box."

"Mom will *never* go for this," says Anthony.

"Duh," I say. "That's why we can't come back here to switch costumes."

"We can change in the garden shed behind my house," says Steven. "Anthony and I will get the extra costumes there ahead of time."

"Perfect."

Will chooses a skeleton costume. Then he goes for the creepy monster mask. He usually doesn't do scary, so I give him a double thumbs-up.

Anthony grabs a clown's wig and

sticks it on his head. "I think you've out-done yourself this time, little brother," he says. "Big-time."

On Sunday morning Dad calls to talk with us.

"I know this is a big night for you, Stuey," he says. "So what are you going to be?"

"A chameleon," I answer without thinking.

"Wow, that sounds neat. What does your costume look like?"

"It's kind of hard to explain," I say.

"Well, be sure to have your mom take a picture. Then you can mail it to me so I can see it. Okay?"

"If there's time. Gotta go. Love you, Dad."

So, how am I gonna figure that out? If I'm lucky, Dad might forget about it. But maybe Mom's camera should get lost somehow.

Anthony and I start getting dressed at five o'clock. I cover my head with my helmet and get my sword. Anthony is Dracula, Will shows up as a wizard, and Steven's a ninja.

"You boys look great," says Mom. "I'd like to take some pictures, but I can't seem to find the camera anywhere. It's not in its usual place. Has anyone seen it? Can you give me a minute to look for it?"

"We don't have a minute, Mom," I say. "We've gotta get going."

"All right then, I know you've been waiting for this all year, Stuey. But remember the rules now, and be safe. Anthony, Steven, I'm counting on you boys to watch out for Stuey and Will. Promise me you'll be responsible."

It's a good thing Anthony has white makeup all over his face, 'cause his neck is turning as red as the fake blood around his fangs.

"Of course we'll be responsible," he mumbles.

And we're off!

Everything goes smoothly. Our bags fill up. We're almost done with our first trip around the block, and then we knock on the door of a yellow house. The house that has loud, creepy music coming out of it and a Just Sold sign on the front lawn.

"Who's there?" calls a familiar voice.

The front door opens. Through the grate in my helmet, I see two red braids.

"Wow! Great costumes, kids," Ms. Curtis says. "Do I know any of you?"

"No," I answer quickly.

"That's not Will under that white beard?" she asks. "Well, you're one cool-looking wizard. Whoever you are."

She smiles as she taps my helmet. "And you must be a *secret* knight. Am I right?"

I don't say a word. Then she gives us each some treats and winks at me before closing the door.

"Wow!" says Will. "I can't believe that Ginger lives in your neighborhood! What are the odds of that happening? How come you didn't tell me? When did she move in?"

My heart is pounding so hard, it feels like it's going to explode.

"She must have just moved in," I say. "We can't go back there again."

"Look, I'm as surprised as you are, Stu. But she's giving out my favorite candy," says Anthony.

"Cool it, Stuey," says Steven. "She didn't know who the three of us are. And even if she recognized Will, he'll be wearing a mask next time."

* * *

We get to Steven's shed and quickly change. I throw the sheet over myself and turn into a ghost. Will puts on the monster mask. Anthony becomes a clown, and Steven turns into an old man.

We start out a second time, and do you know what? The caper works! Everyone gives us candy. All over again! Our bags are getting really heavy. I'm feeling so good, I almost forget about the yellow house and Ms. Curtis. And then we're in front of her door. Again. And I remember.

"Let's forget it," I say.

"Stu, the sheet completely covers you," Anthony says. "Will and Steven have masks on. She won't know me in this nose, wig, and glasses. No one else is giving out root beer barrels and fireballs. Let's go." And before I know it, Anthony grabs my hand and pulls me up the walk. He knocks on the door.

Ms. Curtis opens the door, and we all scream "Trick or treat!"

I hold my breath.

"Wow, those bags look really heavy. You kids are having one great night." She throws a handful of candy in each of our bags. "Have fun," she says. She starts to close the door.

We pulled it off! We really did it! I can't believe I'm safe! *Yes!* And then I hear it. The most annoying voice in the whole world, and it's screaming right behind me.

"Wait a second! Stop! Don't close the door! Trick or treat! Oh, my goodness! I didn't know *you* lived here, Ginger!"

I close my eyes, hoping to wake up

from this horrible nightmare. But when I open them, I'm still standing between two Pippi Longstockings!

Lilly twirls around in a little circle. "See, Ginger, I told you I was going to be Pippi. With braids that curl *up*."

"I can see that," says Ms. Curtis.

I keep perfectly still.

Lilly looks at all of us closely. "Do I know any of you?" she asks.

No one answers. Then she gets up close to Anthony's face. Before he can stop her, she yanks off his clown nose!

"I thought that was you, Anthony Lewis." She looks at the rest of us. "I knew I should have bet you, Stuey," she says, zeroing in on Will. "So you're just a plain old monster, huh? What's so special about that?" And she goes to grab Will's mask.

Ms. Curtis quickly steps out and takes Lilly's hand.

"That's enough, Lilly," she says quietly. She opens up Lilly's fingers and takes the nose from her hand. Then she says, "You know Lilly, you are lucky you didn't bet Stuey. He was already here earlier with Will."

Lilly's mouth drops open. "Are you sure?"

Ms. Curtis gives her a teacher look, the end-of-discussion kind.

She puts some candy in Lilly's bag. "Happy Halloween. I'll see you in school tomorrow." And Lilly takes off.

Then Ms. Curtis puts Anthony's nose back on. She feels my candy bag. "Seems like you have enough loot to last quite a while, don't you think, guys?"

Then she gives a little chuckle, walks

inside, and closes the door. We all look at each other and let out a big breath.

"That was one close call," says Steven. "Maybe we should quit while we're ahead."

"Do you think Ms. Curtis has figured out the caper?" asks Anthony.

"I bet she has," says Will.

"It doesn't matter," I say. "She'll never tell."

And you know what? I won't, either.

Stuey!" Mom yells. "Shake a leg! Anthony's soccer game starts at eleven. We can't be late for warm-up."

I walk outside. Anthony and Steven look plenty warm already. They're wearing shiny lobster red uniforms and bouncing balls off their heads on the driveway.

"Heads up!" I yell.

Anthony and Steven look up. The balls fall.

"Thanks a lot, Stu-pid!" Anthony lunges at me.

"We have to pick up Will!" Mom calls from the door. "Get in the car, guys."

I beat Anthony to the car. I snag the front seat. Maybe I don't play soccer, but I can still score.

"Stuey, one, Anthony, zero," I say. Just to let him know I'm still in the game.

"What's your problem?" Anthony asks. "Why are you acting like a jerk?"

Mom gets in just as the word *jerk* trips off his lips.

"Anthony, you know I don't like that word."

He glares at me, and I whisper, "Stuey, two, Anthony, zero."

At the game people jump up and down and cheer like crazy. "Go, Red! Go, Anthony!" I guess I should tell you now, Anthony is like Mr. Soccer Star. Believe me, it's a big deal. Believe me, it's a big drag. So everyone's screaming but me, even Will. And then the horn blows.

"Did you see his winning goal?" asks Will. "Anthony was awesome."

I've heard it a zillion times. It even used to make *me* proud. But that was before. Before they posted sign-up for bitty league soccer. Anthony's coach comes over to us.

"Great kickoff to the season," Coach Bean says to Mom. "You should be very proud of Anthony." Then he looks at me. "Are you in second grade yet, Stuey?" I nod. He puts his hand on my shoulder. "Sign-up for bitty league soccer is Monday after school." He gives me a wink. "Ready to follow in your big brother's footsteps?"

I don't say a word. Mom stares at me. Will stares at me. Coach Bean stares at me. It's like the whole world's turned into a giant eyeball. It's so scary I have to shut my eyes. Then Will pokes me in the side and it really hurts! My eyes fly open, but my mouth stays shut.

Mom says, "Stuey, Coach Bean asked you a question."

This is it, if I don't answer, I'm in trouble, *big-time*. I take a deep breath, I open my mouth, and then—

Anthony runs up. And everyone looks at *him*. He's all smiles as he asks, "Pretty cool game, huh?"

His timing is perfect. He scores double for this move. Four points, at least!

"Way to go, Anthony!" says Will. He gives him a high five.

"What an exciting game," says Mom.

"Excellent teamwork," says Coach Bean.

I throw my arms around him and hug him tight.

"Great save!" I say.

So here's my question. How can you follow in someone's footsteps when their feet are way bigger than yours? Got any ideas? Me neither.

"Anthony's got pretty big feet," I say to Will at school on Monday.

"So?"

"So, I'm not signing up for soccer."

"Because Anthony's got big feet? I don't get it. You're kidding, right?"

I shake my head no. Will is not happy. I feel bad, but I'm not gonna change my mind.

"That's crazy, Stu. Sign-up is today."

"For you, maybe," I say, "but not for me."

"But we're going to be on the same team, remember?"

"I don't want to play anymore," I say.

"But why?" he asks.

"I just don't," I say.

"Well, that's not good enough," he says. "Does Anthony know?"

"Not yet," I say. "And neither does Mom."

Will stops talking to me. I knew he was gonna be mad. He ignores me at recess and eats lunch with Sam. He ignores me the whole rest of the day, too.

The bell rings. Ms. Curtis says, "It's time to go home, friends. Please get your coats. So, how many of you are planning to sign up for soccer?"

Almost everyone raises a hand. Will stares at me. My hand weighs a ton. I couldn't lift it if I wanted to.

When I get home, Mom is all excited.

"Let's go sign you up, Stu."

"I'm not playing," I say. I go to my room and shut my door.

There's a knock, but before I can yell *Don't come in!* Anthony comes in.

"What's up, Stu?"

"Nothing," I say. "I just don't want to play."

"Why?" he asks.

"Why don't you tap dance?"

He rolls his eyes. "Because I don't want to."

"Well, I don't want to, either."

"Tap dance?"

I roll *my* eyes. "No, lamebrain, play soccer. And I don't want to talk about it. To you *or* Mom, okay?"

"Whatever, Stu." He walks out.

I go to my closet. I pull out Anthony's

soccer cleats from last year, and I slip them on. Two of my feet could fit inside each one. *Easily.*

"Stuey!" Mom calls. "Phone!"

Maybe it's Will. Maybe he's going to forgive me. But it's Dad calling. Our phone dates are on Sundays. We already talked yesterday. Mom must have called him.

"Just go take a walk and think about it. Okay, Stuey?" he asks.

"Okay," I say.

I shuffle around the block in Anthony's cleats. Trust me, it's not easy.

When I get to the yellow house, I stop. Ms. Curtis is out front working in her garden.

"Hey, Stuey, cool cleats!" she calls. "But aren't they a little big? Must be very hard walking around in those."

I nod. "Anthony wore these last year," I say. "But I don't think I'll *ever* fit into them."

She smiles. "Sure you will. I'd bet in three to four years. So, Stuey, tell me something. How long has Anthony been playing soccer?"

I do the math. "Four years, I guess, going on five. He's *wicked* good at it," I tell her.

"I bet he is," she says. "He's been at it a *very long* time. But do you think he was wicked good when he first started?" she asks.

"I never thought about it," I tell her.

"Well, maybe you should," she says. "And while you're at it, maybe you should also try on Anthony's cleats from second grade." She gives me a wink. "I bet they just might fit."

* * *

She's right. Mom dug them up in the basement, and they fit. I think about changing my mind for two whole days. I've almost decided, but I need to ask Anthony something first.

"When you first started playing soccer, were you any good?"

He doesn't even think about it. "I stunk," he says.

After dinner, I call Will. "Do you think there's room for me on Tony's Pizza?"

"I sure hope so," he says. Best friends always forgive each other. "We got our uniforms today. They're orange and really cool. Coach Tucci says every time we win a game, we get free pizza! Have your mom call right away, okay? We have practice after school tomorrow. It's going to be awesome being on the same team!" Will is so excited he can barely catch his breath.

Mom calls, but there's no more room on Will's team. So I ask her to call Sam's coach, but Dee's Deli is full, too. She makes a whole bunch of phone calls.

"They never had so many kids sign up before," she says. "But they promised to get you on a team. Go to bed, Stuey. Don't worry, you'll know by morning."

At breakfast Mom gives me the news.

"There's a brand-new team this year, sponsored by Stan's Chevrolets. You have practice right after school today with Coach Stanley."

"What's a Chevrolet?" I ask.

"It's a type of car."

"Will's team gets free pizza when they

win a game," I say. "Do you think we'll get cars?"

"I don't think so," Mom says.

I walk into my classroom. I can't wait to tell Ms. Curtis and Will. But Lilly is blabbing away nonstop at Ms. Curtis. She's holding a pickle green shirt and acting more obnoxious than usual.

"Isn't this shirt just adorable?" Her voice goes on and on and on.

I wish she'd pipe down so I can talk to Ms. Curtis. I give a couple of those fake coughs, until they finally notice me.

"Stuey!" Lilly screams. She waves the shirt at me. "Stuey! You're on my soccer team!"

She's completely lost it. I almost feel sorry for her, but not quite.

"No I'm not," I tell her.

And then she flips over into know-it-all mode.

"See for yourself," she says. She holds up the green shirt, and it says STAN'S CHEVROLETS on the back.

After school, I try to talk Mom into letting me quit. She won't. I tell her about Lilly, but she doesn't get it.

"How annoying can one girl be?" She winks at me. "You know how to deal with Anthony. Just ignore her." She drops me off at practice.

I look around. Ignore Lilly? Maybe, but what I can't ignore is this: almost everyone on the field is a girl. The good news is, Lilly's not one of them. Maybe she quit. A lady blows a whistle.

"Take a lap, everybody!"

We start running around the field. Man, some of these girls can really fly. I kick it up a notch and run as hard as I can. Five girls finish before me, *and* one boy.

He comes up to me. "Hi, I'm Arthur."

"Stuey," I say. "What's with all the girls?"

"There weren't enough girls to start their own league. So Stan's Chevrolets decided to sponsor this team."

I get to the point. "Any other boys?"

"One," said Arthur, "but he quit. You're not going to quit, are you?"

"My mom won't let me," I say.

He points to the lady with the whistle. "Mine won't, either."

"Your mom's Coach Stanley?"

"No, my mom's the assistant coach. There's Coach Stanley." He points to a pickle green car pulling into the lot. A large man gets out and starts jogging over to the rest of us.

"Sorry I'm late," he says to Arthur's mother. Then he looks at me. "You must be Stuey Lewis. Welcome to Stan's Chevrolets. My daughter has told me all about you."

Daughter? I look at all the girls in front of me. I don't know any of them, and I start feeling a little strange. And

then I hear that voice, like fingernails scraping down a chalkboard.

"Dad! Wait up, Dad! You better not start without me, Dad!" And there's Lilly, running at top speed. Straight at me!

I think about running in the opposite direction, but Coach Stanley clamps a big hand down on my shoulder. It's wicked heavy. I'm not going anywhere anytime soon.

"Check out her form!" he says, pointing at Lilly and pounding my back. "That's our girl," he tells me with a proud smile.

I don't smile back.

Lilly almost mows me down. "I told you we were on the same team, didn't I, Stuey Lewis?" she says. "We can start now, Dad, I'm good to go."

I hear Mom's words inside my head: *Just ignore her. How annoying can one girl be?* Well, I've got news for you: plenty. But pretty soon I see that Mom is right. I don't have time to think about anything, including Lilly Stanley. I'm way too busy learning how to play soccer, *and* I'm following in Anthony's footsteps. Just like when he first started, I stink, too.

"Don't be a ball hog, Lewis! Pass it!"

yells Angel. She's the best player on the team. I pass it over to her. "Nice pass!" she yells, then she kicks the ball. It sails through the air and lands neatly in the goal. I'm not gonna be the star of *this* team, *ever.* Let me just get through the season, without looking too stupid.

"Heads up!" *Wham!* A ball crashes into my gut. Suddenly, I'm flat on the ground and I feel like I'm gonna lose lunch. I look up and see the whole team looking down at me.

"Don't move, Stuey," says Coach Stanley. "Are you okay?"

"You're not going to quit, are you?" asks Arthur.

"Hey, Lewis, nice save!" says Angel. She points to my hands. "You're still holding on to the ball. You're like a natural goalie. Way to go, Stu!"

I stand up even though I feel a little woozy.

"Shake it off!" says Angel.

I shake, and everyone starts clapping, even Lilly. They put me in goal.

"You've got to have that no-fear attitude, son," says Coach Stanley.

Son? If I were his son, then Lilly would be my sister! *Eek!* That scares me plenty.

"Earth to Stuey. Are you listening?" He gives me a little shake.

I nod. "No fear," I say.

"And be aggressive. Goalies have to be aggressive, tough, alert, and on guard at all times. Remember, keep your eye on the ball. Never let it in the goal. Never, got it?"

I nod. But to tell you the truth, what I've really got is a wicked bellyache.

Coach Stanley blows his whistle.

"Everybody, line up behind the penalty line." He gives each kid a ball. "Okay, guys, Stuey's going to try to block each of your shots." I try not to look like I'm gonna throw up. "Angel, you're up first."

She kicks too hard, and the ball flies over the net. Arthur's next, and I block his shot. Balls shoot at me, but I get into a rhythm, and guess what? I do okay. I miss a few, but mostly I don't. And then it's Lilly's turn, and she kicks one right into my face.

"Oops!" she says. I drop the ball as Mom honks the horn. End of first practice. Final score, Lilly, 1, Stuey, 0.

It's a double whammy: it's our first game *and* we're playing Tony's Pizza. Will's team, the dream team that could have been *my* team. I look at them.

They're all in orange and they're all boys. They get pizza when they win and they don't have to ignore Lilly Stanley. The thought of pizza makes my stomach roll. I bet my face looks as green as my shirt. My hands begin shaking, and I can't get my goalie gloves on.

"It takes a lot of guts to be a goalie." Anthony is suddenly beside me. "I couldn't do it, but I know you can, Stu. So go for it!" He high-fives me, and I feel a little better, until the whistle blows. Now I'm all alone in the box.

"Go, Orange! Go, Green!" Everyone's screaming, even me.

Most of the action is at the other end of the field. "Go, Angel! Go, Green!" I cheer.

Angel scores the first goal. I wonder how *their* goalie's feeling. I find out soon enough, when I miss the shot. Game's tied. Orange, 1, Green, 1.

"Keep your eyes on the ball, Stu!" Coach Stanley gives me a pep talk. "Be aggressive!"

My eyes are glued to the ball. I try feeling aggressive, but I only feel scared.

Twenty kids charge the net. I wave my arms. I run back and forth. The ball comes flying at me . . . I hold my breath . . . I catch it!

"Go, Stuey! Great save!" The crowd is screaming.

I'm unstoppable! I kick the ball to Arthur. He passes to Angel. She races toward the other goal. My heart slows down, but just a little. Being a goalie takes a lot out of you.

The game's almost over. The score's still tied, and then they charge the net again. Arthur is in the box, trying to block the ball. It hits his hand, and the whistle shrieks.

"Hand ball! Penalty kick! Thirty seconds left!" shouts the ref.

Everyone is quiet. Will is at the penalty line. He looks at me, and I look back at him. Then I look at the ball, and I'm sure of one thing. *No way* is that ball getting past me. I will not miss this shot, *I will not*. Then everything seems to melt away, and all that is left is me, Will, and the ball.

Then he kicks. It's the perfect shot. It sails way over my head. I jump higher than I've ever jumped before, but not high enough. Will scores.

The horn blows. "Yay, Will! Yay, Orange!" People are cheering. The other team is jumping up and down like crazy.

"Pretty lucky shot," says Will. He puts his hand up for a high five.

"Pretty *amazing* shot," I answer. Our hands slap, and then we are both surrounded by our teams.

"Great job, Stu," says Coach Stanley. "You really took the heat."

"There was no way to save that shot, Lewis," says Angel.

"Awesome try," says Arthur.

Lilly nods.

I know that everything they say is true.

Anthony's Coach Bean comes up to us as we're leaving the field.

"Great kickoff to the season," he says as he puts his arm around my shoulder. He looks at Mom. "You should be very proud of Stuey."

"Oh, I am," says Mom.

Then he leans down and gives me a wink. "Guess you're following in your brother's footsteps after all."

"He's got his own feet," says Anthony.

I smile. He ought to know, he's my big brother.

I have a confession to make. I'm not so hot with endings. I'm not so hot with beginnings, either, but at least with beginnings you don't know what to expect. With endings you know what you're going to miss. So, okay, the last day of school is supposed to be exciting, right? And though I love summer vacation as much as any kid, this year feels kind of different. I don't want to say goodbye to Ginger and all the good things that happened to me, like becoming a good reader. I guess this year I wouldn't mind postponing summer another month, just in case I'm not gonna like my third-grade teacher so much.

When Dad calls Sunday afternoon to check in and says, "Last day of school is in three days, Stu. You must be pretty excited, huh?" I don't answer him.

"Stuey, did you hear me?"

"Yes, Dad, I heard you."

But I can't tell him that I think the last day of school stinks. 'Cause if he thinks I'm not excited about summer starting on time, he might think I don't want to go on our camping trip.

I can't say a word to Anthony, either. 'Cause he's totally psyched about the end of the school year and summer starting on time.

I give Will a call.

"Hey, Will. How do you feel about the last day of school?"

"Well, it's not as cool as Halloween and *definitely* not Hanukkah. It's cooler than the first day, because then you have a whole year of school ahead of you. But actually, by the end of the summer you're getting kind of bored and looking forward to having school start again, so maybe the first day is cooler than the last day after all."

Will is a thinker. If I don't stop him, he'll go on about this for a whole hour. So I cut to the chase.

"I'm thinking about skipping it this year," I say.

"How come?" he asks.

"Just because."

And because he doesn't ask "Just because, why?" I tell him.

The next morning, Will stops me at the classroom door. "It's a little naked in there," he warns. I walk in.

A *little* naked? It barely looks like

our room. "Those Lazy, Hazy, Crazy Days of Summer" is blasting out of the CD player. Ms. Curtis must have spent the whole weekend stripping everything down.

"Please come to meeting!" she calls. "Let's read the morning message together."

Happy Monday!
Only three days until
our last day together.
I have a surprise for you.
Let's share about the weekend.
Then we'll talk about the surprise.
XO,
Ginger

"We certainly know what *you* did this weekend, Ginger," Lilly gushes. "You're so on top of things, but the room does look kind of sad."

Kind of sad? It makes *me* want to throw up.

"And do you know what else, Ginger? *I* have a surprise, too," Lilly says. "My birthday is on Wednesday! I guess that makes the last day of school extra special, don't you think? So the whole class can celebrate me and the beginning of summer at the same time!" Lilly smiles up at Ms. Curtis.

Now I'm *really* gonna throw up. And my decision is final; the last day of school will definitely happen *without* me.

"Thanks for sharing, Lilly," says Ms. Curtis. "So, who's got weekend news? How many of you did summer things?"

"We cleaned out our camper all weekend," says Nathan.

"We went to the lake," says Sam.

"I went fishing," says Rosa.

"I got a new swimsuit," says Sashi.

"We got a new grill," says Omar.

"I thought about school," I say.

Lilly looks at me like I'm from another planet.

"My mother will be making all of us cupcakes for my birthday," Lilly blabs on. "With pink frosting and little flowers on top. *And* she's sending in watermelon sherbet. That's my *second* surprise. What's your surprise, Ginger?"

"Well, just before it's time to go home today, we'll be choosing Secret Friends," says Ms. Curtis. "You'll do special things for your Secret Friend for two days. But you can't let the person know who you are. It's a secret until our end-of-the-year party on Wednesday."

"That sounds very exciting, Ginger," Lilly says. "I hope I get you."

"Remember, it's a secret. We will all be picking names out of a hat," says Ms. Curtis. "And I want to make one thing clear. There will be no complaining. You will be nice to whoever your Secret Friend is. Understand?"

We all nod. Then I raise my hand.

"And *everyone* has to take part in this." She looks straight at me.

I put my hand down. Since I'm not showing up on Wednesday, I guess I can handle being nice for one day. How bad could it be?

Wicked bad. Actually, worse than wicked bad. What's worse than wicked bad? A slip of paper that says *Lilly Stanley*! And guess who pulled it out of the hat? This can't be happening to me!

"Remember what we talked about this morning," Ms. Curtis says. "No one should be making faces. No one should be making noises."

I look around the room. I try not to look at Lilly. Nobody seems that unhappy. 'Cause nobody has to be nice to Lilly Stanley. Except me. For *one whole day*!

"Do not tell anyone who your Secret Friend is," says Ms. Curtis.

"Not even your mom?" asks Sam.

"You can tell your parents," says Ms. Curtis. "But no one else, okay? So let's brainstorm some ideas we can do for our Secret Friends."

"You could hide a special snack in their cubby," says Sashi.

"You could do nice things for them," says Will.

"You could make sure they have someone to play with at recess," says Nathan.

"You could give them something you made," says Lilly.

"You could send them to China," I say. "For a *very* long time."

Ms. Curtis frowns. Some of the kids laugh.

"China's a big country," I say. "It'd take a *very* long time to see it." I try to look innocent. The bell rings.

"Think about what you can do tomorrow for your Secret Friend," says Ms. Curtis. "And re-

member, no telling. Have a great afternoon."

Then she whispers to me, "Stuey, I'd
like to speak with you."

"Me, too," I say. We wait till everyone
is gone.

"This Secret Friend thing," I say. "It's
gonna be hard for me."

"Want to talk about it?"

"I really don't like my Secret Friend."

"I'm sorry, Stuey. It would be more
fun if you did. But it *is* possible to be
nice to someone who you don't like."
She gives me a smile. "It might be hard,
but you can do it."

"Maybe, but I'll tell you what I can't
do. I can't celebrate the last day of
school, 'cause I think it's stupid and I totally won't do it!" I'm almost yelling. And
then, before I know it, I tell her about

not wanting the school year to end. I tell her how I'm gonna skip the last day and that I'm big-time nervous about my next year's teacher.

She puts her arm around me. "Stuey," she says, "everyone's always a bit nervous about endings, and beginnings, too. You should have seen me the week before school started. I was a wreck."

"I guess," I say. "But you don't look like a wreck now that it's ending."

She gives me a little squeeze. "Look, Stuey, I promise that the end of this year and the beginning of next are going to be just fine. And I'd really like it if you'd come on the last day. There's another surprise I have for all of you, and I don't think you should miss it. So just think about it, okay?"

"Okay," I say. And then I tell her about Lilly.

"Trust me, Stu, you'll survive. I know you'll make this work."

Will calls after dinner. "Have you made a decision about the last day of school?" he asks.

"Yeah, I'm gonna go."

"Cool," he says. "Have you figured out what you're going to do for your Secret Friend tomorrow?" he asks.

"I don't want to talk about it."

"Yeah, I know we're not supposed to."

"I mean I *really* don't want to talk about it."

"Is it that bad?" he asks.

"Even worse," I say. "But it's only for two days."

I go downstairs. I look through the kitchen drawers. I dig up a pair of chopsticks. I find some wrapped fortune cookies from our last dinner at the Golden Dragon. I even find a red paper fan. Maybe I can't really send Lilly to China, but I can sure pretend.

"What are you doing with all that stuff?" Mom asks.

I tell her about Lilly.

"You know, I've got a little

teapot. You could take that, too."

"Awesome," I say.

The next morning, I get to class before Lilly. I hide the fortune cookies in her cubby. I can't wait till she finds them. "Sunshine and Summertime" is playing on the CD player. We're all sneaking around, and everyone is smiling. Maybe this isn't so stupid after all.

"Fortune cookies! I got fortune cookies in my cubby, Ginger!" Lilly's jumping up and down. "I bet I know who my Secret Friend is!" She looks around the room, ready to pounce on her Secret Friend.

I duck my head. My face is so red it could be sunburned.

"Remember the rules now, Lilly." Ms. Curtis uses her no-nonsense voice. "We're not saying anything about who our Secret Friend is until our party tomorrow."

"It's okay, Ginger," says Lilly in her most obnoxious voice. "I won't say her name."

I look up. Her name? *Her* name? Lilly's not even looking at me. She's looking straight at Sashi! Sashi, who thought of hiding a special snack in a cubby. Sashi, whose family comes from China! Lilly thinks Sashi's her Secret Friend. *Yes!* I'm still in the game.

At snack time there's a chocolate cupcake on my desk. Will gets a bookmark. He gives me a thumbs-up. "Summer in the City" is playing on the CD player.

"Ginger!" Lilly yells. "Both of my fortune cookies say I'm in for a big surprise! Do *you* have any idea what that means, Sashi?"

"No," says Sashi.

Well, I sure do, Ms. Know-It-All. And you're gonna feel plenty dumb when you find out.

"Hey, Stu, want to play four square at recess?" asks Omar.

"Sure," I say.

"Let's ask Sashi and Nathan, too," he says.

Out on the playground, everybody's playing.

"Stuey." Lilly comes up to me. "Do you think you could get our basketball down? It's stuck between the rim and the backboard."

"Sure," I say. I throw a perfect shot, sinking their ball and mine through the hoop. Then I hand Lilly's back to her.

"Thanks," she says, giving me a smile. "You are such a big help."

"Say cheese!" says Ms. Curtis. She snaps our picture and gives me a wink. "This is a moment I sure want to remember," she says.

"Could I have a copy of that picture,

Ginger?" Lilly asks. "Maybe you'd like a copy, too, Stuey?"

"Uh, I've got to go to the bathroom," I say. I run into school and go to my classroom. I hide the fan in Lilly's desk. I put the chopsticks in her lunch box. And then I see it! It's taped to my cubby. A gift certificate for a brownie sundae at Scoops!

"I really lucked out," I tell Will. "I've got the best Secret Friend ever."

"I guess the end-of-the-year thing is working for you," he says.

"Yeah," I say. "It's actually not so bad."

I wake up early the next morning. I get my stuff ready for Lilly. Some tea and the little china teapot Mom had. Then I have an idea. I pull out my markers and get to work.

Mom walks in. "What are you making?"

"Something extra for Lilly," I say.

At school everyone's all excited. Lilly finds the teapot and the tea. She still thinks Sashi's her Secret Friend. I get a mini squirt gun and a bag of chips. I feel good, better than good. So I decide to give Lilly the extra something. I hand her the card after lunch.

She reads it out loud.

"Roses are red,
Violets are blewis—

Blewis? What kind of a word is *blewis?"*

Her voice gets all screechy. My face gets all hot. Ms. Curtis suddenly looks nervous.

Then Lilly smiles. "Oh, how cute!" She starts again.

"Roses are red,
Violets are blewis,
Happy birthday to you,
Signed, Stuey Lewis

Thank you, Stuey," she says. "This is really nice."

Ms. Curtis smiles at me. Will looks at me like I'm nuts. Maybe I am, but being nice feels pretty good. Even to Lilly, for two whole days.

"Well, it's time for our party," says Ms. Curtis. "Have you all enjoyed having Secret Friends?"

"Yes!" we all yell.

"Is it time to find out who they are?"

"Yes!" we yell again.

"All right then. But before we do, I've got a special secret to share. I now can tell each of you who your next year's teacher is going to be."

Everyone suddenly goes silent.

"I hope you'll all be as happy as I was when I found out that this whole class will be together again next year with me as your teacher."

"But that's not possible, Ginger," Lilly says. "That's not how it works."

"You're right, Lilly, it hasn't worked that way before. But since both of the third-grade teachers are leaving this year, the school has decided to have Ms. Plum and me keep our same classes for next year. Looks like we'll all be together again in third grade. I hope that works for everybody," she says, looking straight at me.

I give her a double thumbs-up as everyone breaks into cheers.

"Okay then," says Ms. Curtis. "Back to the other secret at hand. If you think you know, you may ask the person you think is your Secret Friend."

"I know who you are!" screams Lilly. She runs right up to Sashi. "I've known from the very first clue on the very first day that you are definitely my very own Secret Friend, Sashi Liang."

"Well, I'm not your Secret Friend," says Sashi.

"You have to tell the truth now, Sashi Liang! Doesn't she, Ginger?"

Lilly's face has gone tomato red.

"I *am* telling you the truth," says Sashi. "I am *not* your Secret Friend."

"But, you *have* to be," says Lilly in a

quiet voice. She looks like she's gonna cry. She looks like she feels really dumb.

"Hey, Lilly," I say. "Remember what your fortune cookies said about a big surprise?" I ask. "Well, guess what? I'm the big surprise. I'm your Secret Friend."

Her mouth drops open. "But you can't be, Stuey Lewis," she says.

"Why not?" I ask.

"Because you're mine!"

"No way!" I say.

She nods. And then everyone starts clapping.

"Wow," says Will, looking back and forth between me and Lilly. "This is unbelievable. It's almost like a movie."

"Don't push it," I say.

But I smile. Me and Lilly spent two whole days being nice to each other.

And you know what? We're still alive. Happy ending? You bet!

Now, next year's another story, but Ginger's right, I'll survive. I can make *anything* work.

SQUARE FISH

DISCUSSION GUIDE

THE ONE AND ONLY STUEY LEWIS

by Jane Schoenberg

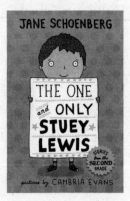

Discussion Questions

1. Which story do you like best? Why?

2. How are your classroom and school week the same as Stuey's? How are they different?

3. Have you ever had a favorite teacher? What did you like about him or her? What makes Ginger special?

4. Have you ever had any of the same fears or struggles as Stuey? Talk (or write) about what you did, or can do, to deal with them.

5. Talk (or write) about something (sports, school, art, or music, for example) that's been easy for you. Talk (or write) about something that's been challenging.

6. What do you think of Stuey and Anthony's relationship? Talk (or write) about the benefits and challenges of having a sibling.

7. If you could choose one character from this book to visit your classroom for a day, whom would you pick, and why? How are you different from, or similar to, this character?

8. What do you think of Lilly? Do you think she'll be different in third grade? Why or why not?

9. If you could choose a secret friend to be nice to, whom would you pick? Make a list of things you might do for and with that person.

GOFISH

QUESTIONS FOR THE AUTHOR

JANE SCHOENBERG

© Ryan Jensen

What did you want to be when you grew up?
My dream was to be on Broadway because I loved to sing and dance, and I had a great passion for musicals. I collected Broadway cast albums and memorized all the lyrics to every song. Then one day when I was sixteen, I watched a PBS program about Down syndrome kids, and I fell in love with them. I started a camp program for special needs kids that summer with my town's parks and recreation department, and I decided to become a teacher. Music and kids have always been important parts of my life. They still are.

Were you a reader or a non-reader growing up?
Like Will, I was always a voracious reader. I went to the library once a week and came home with seven books, one for each day of the week! My parents belonged to the Book-of-the-Month Club, and when I was a little older I read their books, too. In sixth grade, I got

to be a librarian's helper once a week. I loved stamping the due dates on the cards, and being in charge of hundreds of books for an hour was blissful. I didn't mind missing math class, either.

When did you realize you wanted to be a writer?
I didn't realize I wanted to be a writer until I was much older, although when I look back on my life, I was always writing something—like poetry, song lyrics, narratives, and scripts. I always loved to write, and it always felt comfortable. I spent several years teaching kids how to read and write, and to perform onstage. During those years, I began to get serious about writing children's books.

What's your most embarrassing childhood memory?
I was at an amusement park and had to go to the bathroom. I was in a bit of a hurry and entered the men's room instead of the women's. Thank goodness no one was in there, but I was really mortified that people might see me on my way out!

What's your favorite childhood memory?
I went to overnight camp for many summers in the beautiful Berkshires of Massachusetts. I loved my time away at camp. I had a whole set of camp friends whom I wrote letters to, all winter long. We couldn't wait to get back together in July. The camp was on a lake and nestled in the woods, with special hideaway places like the pine grove and inspiration rock.

What was your favorite thing about school?
I loved being with my friends. I was always very social, and lucky to have a nice group of kids to hang out with. English was my favorite class, because we dug deep into books. I had this fabulous sixth-grade teacher, Mr. Margeson, who really challenged us. We read classics with him, like Dickens's *A Tale of Two Cities*, and we studied poetry. He introduced us to onomatopoeia,* iambic pentameter** (aren't those wonderful-sounding words?), and great literature that year. I was hooked!

*words that sound like the sound they make, like *buzz*, *hiss*, and *pop*

a rhythm that sounds like ba-bum**, ba-**bum**, ba-**bum**, ba-**bum**, ba-**bum**

What was your least favorite thing about school?
I would have to say math class, and home economics in middle school. The half year when everyone learned to cook was fun, but the rest of the year when *almost* everyone learned to sew was torture. I flunked wash-cloth slippers. (I know, who would even think to make slippers out of washcloths, right?) The apron and skirt were even more traumatic. To this day, the thought of sitting in front of a sewing machine gives me a stom-achache.

What were your hobbies as a kid? What are your hobbies now?
When I was a kid, I spent most of my time listening to music, reading, and being with my friends. But those were more like staples in my life than hobbies. I still do

those things today, and I garden. I spend hours getting lost in my flower gardens, which keep me grounded and connected to butterflies, bees, and hummingbirds.

What was your first job, and what was your "worst" job?
My first job was babysitting. I used to get a dollar an hour, even when there were three kids to take care of. No worst job—I've been extremely lucky that I've loved all the jobs I've had. I've always worked with children.

What book is on your nightstand now?
It just so happens that we have a *brand*-new baby granddaughter, Sofie Beatrice, whom we're going to meet this weekend. So I have a pile of books for her: Eric Carle's *Papa, Please Get the Moon for Me*, Margaret Wise Brown's *Runaway Bunny*, Mem Fox's *Time for Bed*, and my book *The Baby Hustle* are just a few.

How did you celebrate publishing your first book?
The first book was called *My Bodyworks*, which I wrote with my husband, Steven. It comes with a CD of twelve songs that teach kids about their bodies. We had a band that did a small book tour, and we celebrated by putting on our first performance for the kids in our town.

Where do you write your books?
I usually write upstairs in our son's old bedroom, which is now my studio. My desk overlooks one of my gardens and an old stone wall. At different times of the

year I see wild turkeys, deer, foxes, and coyotes. Sometimes in the spring, summer, or fall months, I'll take my computer and write on our front porch. I love to do this when the privet bushes are in bloom, when they are filled with hundreds of buzzing bees and a pair of hummingbirds. It's kind of like being in a tree house, only on the ground.

What sparked your imagination for *The One and Only Stuey Lewis*?
I wanted to write a series for young readers. I read a lot of series that were out there, and most of them had a girl protagonist, so I knew I wanted to write about a boy. Then one day I heard this voice in my head saying, "I wake up and decide to have a stomachache that's so bad I have to stay in bed." Stuey had arrived. . . .

What is your favorite Halloween costume?
True confession: I don't dress up for Halloween anymore. But I do have a really cool old tuxedo jacket with sequins on the lapels and a top hat that I wear when I'm doing a reading of *The Great Halloween Caper.*

Have you ever had a secret friend?
I've never had a secret friend, but when I was really little I had an imaginary one. His name was Roger, and he took the rap for all of my ill deeds. "I didn't spill my milk, Roger did. Oh, I can't eat those green things on my plate because they're for Roger. Roger's scared to go to bed, so I need to stay up with him." Get the picture?

What challenges do you face in the writing process, and how do you overcome them?

Much of my work is voice driven, with the protagonist telling the story in his or her own voice. On good days I just move aside and let the character tell the story. On not-so-good days, when I'm stuck, I make myself sit in front of the computer and usually reread and tweak everything I have up to that point. If nothing comes through after that, I'll turn to something else I'm working on, or leave the work altogether and go for a walk, weed the gardens, stack wood, etc. The place where I'm stuck is never too far from my mind, however. Song lyrics particularly haunt me. Like jigsaw puzzles, every syllable has to be an exact fit, and when they don't, I think about it relentlessly.

Which of your characters is most like you?

Ginger Curtis, definitely, and a little bit of Stuey, too. But Lilly is my favorite. She is so outrageous, she makes me laugh out loud.

What makes you laugh out loud?

Besides Lilly? My husband, Steven, who can make just about anybody laugh out loud.

What do you do on a rainy day?

If it clears enough for the sun to make an appearance while it's still raining, I stop whatever I'm doing (even if I'm in the car), go outside, and look in the opposite direction of the sun for a rainbow. I see quite a few of them because I always do this. Try it next time, and you may see one, too.

What was your favorite book when you were a kid? Do you have a favorite book now?

Hmm . . . I had so many favorites. As a young kid I would have to say the Mary Poppins series by P. L. Travers, and, of course, all the classics like *Little Women*, *Heidi*, *Charlotte's Web*, *The World of Pooh* (as in *Winnie-the-Pooh!*), and many more. I kept every one of them, and they are still on my bookshelves.

What do you want readers to remember about your books?

I hope that young readers will relate to Stuey and his experiences, laugh out loud at his antics, and maybe have some conversations about feelings that may not be so easy to express. I'd like kids to remember that they, just like Stuey, will survive experiences that may initially feel daunting.

What would you do if you stopped writing?

I don't think that's ever going to happen.

What do you consider to be your greatest accomplishment?

Helping to raise my two extraordinary children, Sarah Kate Jackson, who is an actor, and Adam Schoenberg, who is a composer. They are both very accomplished artists, and two of my very closest friends.

What do you wish you could do better?
I wish I could do everything better, because no matter how good you are at something, there's always more to learn.

What would your readers be most surprised to learn about you?
They might not know that I am a lyricist, and that I collaborate with my husband, who is an amazing composer. We've written many songs together, lots of them for kids. We're working on several projects. There may be a Stuey musical in the mix!

GOFISH

CAMBRIA EVANS

© Kari Christensen

What did you want to be when you grew up?
I always wanted to be an artist, but the exact kind changed over the years. From sixth grade until college I was set on being a photographer. From there I wanted to be a printmaker, collage artist, and then a graphic designer and illustrator. I love illustrating because I can use all the things I learned from other disciplines and apply them to my artwork.

What's your favorite childhood memory?
Building forts in trees, vacant lots, my backyard, and my bedroom. I loved making forts!

How did you celebrate publishing your first book?
Eating food-truck tacos and riding a street carnival Ferris wheel.

Where do you work on your illustrations?
On a small round table in my tiny New York City apartment.

Where do you find inspiration for your illustrations?
Traveling and people watching in Central Park.

What makes you laugh out loud?
Sloths, snoring dormice, and squeaking guinea pigs.

Who is your favorite fictional character?
Roald Dahl's Matilda.

What's your favorite TV show or movie?
Anything magical or funny.

If you were stranded on a desert island, who would you want for company?
My husband, Kari.

If you could travel in time, where would you go and what would you do?
Edwardian London. I would go shopping for lace-up boots, jewelry, and paper ephemera.

What do you like best about yourself?
My ability to imagine.

What do you wish you could do better?
Math.

What was your favorite thing about school?
Reading new books.

What was your least favorite thing about school?
Cafeteria food.

If you could travel anywhere in the world, where would you go and what would you do?
Paris. I would sit in outdoor cafés, eat gluten-free crêpes, and go to flea markets.

Who is your favorite artist?
Jill Barklem, the illustrator of Brambly Hedge.

What is your favorite medium to work in?
Mixed media—a combination of collage, watercolor, pencil, ink, and digital.

What was your favorite book or comic/graphic novel when you were a kid?
The Arabel and Mortimer series by Joan Aiken.

What's your current favorite?
Jonathan Strange and Mr. Norrell by Susanna Clarke.

What were your hobbies as a kid?
Making stationery and friendship bracelets, creating secret languages or codes, and eating candy.

SQUARE FISH

What are your hobbies now, aside from illustrating?
Designing stationery and accessories, learning languages, and baking sweets.

What challenges do you face in the artistic process, and how do you overcome them?
I get obsessive about tiny details and rendering little things. To help me relax and focus on the big picture, I listen to audio books or have TV on in the background so I am ever-so-slightly distracted.

Stuey Lewis faces new challenges in third grade.
Can he figure out how to transport his class to space,
navigate an airplane trip disaster, and find an awesome
animal for the class pet show?

Find out in
STUEY LEWIS
AGAINST all ODDS

Fuel tanks full . . . Booster rockets set . . . Crew standing by . . . Systems are all cleared and ready to go. Prepare to launch," I tell Will Fishman, my best friend and first mate.

One of the coolest things about third grade, besides having Ginger Curtis as our teacher for the second year in a row, and studying space, is having a humongous table full of Legos in our classroom.

"Five, four, three, two, one, zero . . . *Lift off!*" me and Will shout together as our spacecraft leaves the launchpad and quickly soars upward.

Our mission:

* ★ To explore the mysteries of the cosmos.
* ★ To discover new life-forms on other planets.
* ★ To dare to go where no one's ever gone before.

"Ginger! Stuey and Will have been at the Lego table for eighteen and a half minutes now, and there are only ninety seconds of morning recess left. Plus, they've used up all the rocket pieces from the new Lego set, so no one else can make a spaceship."

And one of the worst things about third grade, besides tons of homework and having to learn cursive, which I stink at, is that I *still* have to put up with having the Queen of Obnoxious in my class. I cross my eyes and look at Lilly Stanley. She has two heads and four eyes. Blab-blab-blabs are coming out of her two mouths, and she has morphed into the most annoying alien ever known to humankind in *any* galaxy.

I pick up my Lego laser and wave it at her.

"You know you're not allowed to make guns at school, Stuey Lewis," she blabs on.

"It's not a gun," Will explains. "It's a frezlien, a highly specialized tool designed to freeze aliens for five minutes, without causing bodily harm, while we collect scientific data from them."

"I guess you and I are safe then, Lilly," says Ms. Curtis, chuckling. "Nice-looking rocket, guys. I'm glad you're psyched about our space unit. We'll talk more

about what we'll be studying later, during science. Lilly, I bet if it's still raining, the boys will be happy to have you join them at the Lego table after lunch. Isn't that right, Stuey?" she asks me.

"The forecast said there's a seventy percent chance of the rain ending before

noon," Will reports, giving me a look that says, Keep your fingers crossed and start wishing for sunshine, pronto.

"Friends, it's time to clean up and get ready for math," Ms. Curtis says. "Want to help pass out the multiplication-mad minute, Lilly?"

"Oh, I'd love to, Ginger."

And *whoosh* . . . Just like that, Lilly's out of *my* space.

Math rocks this year 'cause I happen to be killer at it. So far, I'm the only one with perfect multiplication-mad-minute scores in the *whole* class. But I don't hold it over anybody's head like a certain somebody else might. 'Cause it wasn't so long ago that reading wasn't a piece of cake, and I can tell you that was *not* a whole lot of fun.

But . . . $4 \times 7 = 28$, $3 \times 9 = 27$, and $5 \times 12 = 60$ takes my mind off rain and maybe having to share the Lego table with that certain somebody else, which, trust me, is a very good thing . . . even if it does only last for sixty seconds.